YOUTH WRITERS CHALLENGE SERIES, VOL 6

ADVENTURES OF THE ANTLUZ SUPERHEROES

Ann Taylor, Benjamin Lopez,
Dylan Turner, Kaylani Turner

publish
your gift

ADVENTURES OF THE ANTLUZ SUPERHEROES

Published by Publish Your Gift®
An imprint of Purposely Created Publishing Group, LLC

Printed in the United States of America

ISBN: 978-1-64484-653-7 (print)
ISBN: 978-1-64484-654-4 (ebook)

Special discounts are available on bulk quantity purchases by book clubs, associations and special interest groups. For details email: sales@publishyourgift.com or call (888) 949-6228.
For information logon to: www.PublishYourGift.com

AUTHORS

Benjamin Lopez

Ann Taylor

Dylan Turner

Kaylani Turner

*Thank you to everyone who has supported
the Youth Writers Challenge, Inc. and the
Youth Writers Rock organizations.*

*Thank you to the instructors
who helped with this project:
Patricia Johnson-Harris, Roger Harris,
Lazaria Foreman, Robin Stokes, Jackie JC Gardner,
Debrayta Salley, Jackie Anderson,
Nanette Buchannan, Pam Reaves, Rod Lopez,
Robyn F. Evans, and Joy Turner.*

TABLE OF CONTENTS

PREFACE

The question always arises about whether there are other life forces living amongst us or on other planets. We've been convinced that there are no beings other than those who live here on Earth. But many months ago, a strange flying object entered Earth's atmosphere and it arrived undetected. Why? Because it looked like a shooting star among the planets and as soon as it appeared it disappeared into the corn fields of a small town outside of Orlando, Florida. It left a hole the size of ten basketballs and it scorched the ground so that nothing could ever grow there again.

Particles of metal were scattered for miles, and no one knew that all the broken pieces were part of a larger one, so the mystery remained as one not to be solved. Every time the rain came, all the mud, rocks, and sand filled the hole. Soon the strange flying object was no longer able to be seen. But at night during certain times of the year, it glowed a bright yellow with neon blue streaks.

A few of the brave students at Antluz Middle School had no idea how this would impact their lives and change history forever.

Chapter 1

THE CREW

Benjamin Lopez, Ann Taylor, Dylan Turner,
Kaylani Turner

Who would have thought four middle school students from Parkville, Maryland, would be on the news in Orlando, Florida, and Baltimore, Maryland, at the same time? They called themselves "The Crew"—Kyonn, Tycho, Sophia, and Mya. The four friends lived in the same neighborhood, and their houses were just doors from one another in Parkville, Maryland.

Kyonn and Mya grew up on LaSalle Road in Parkville. Mya and her family lived at 2614 LaSalle Road and Kyonn lived just a few doors down at 2620 LaSalle Road. They had known each other since kindergarten.

When Kyonn and Mya were in the third grade, Tycho moved right across the street from Mya. Tycho lived with his mother and two siblings. It didn't take very long for Tycho to come across the street and introduce himself to

Kyonn when he saw Kyonn outside his house bouncing a basketball, trying to do some Kyrie Irving moves. And just in case you live under a rock, Kyrie Irving just happens to be one of the best players, of our time, in the NBA. Tycho was the oldest of his siblings and the only boy, so he was excited to see another boy his age that he could hang with.

The last of the crew, Sophia, lived one block down. Sophia had lived on LaSalle Road for only three months when she met Mya at school in the fifth grade. Sophia came into the classroom and Mya waved so that Sophia would come over and sit by her.

Meet Kyonn

Kyonn's house was big. It had three floors, a lot of bedrooms, and a basement where Kyonn's dad had a big TV on the wall, big speakers, video games, and a pool table. All the neighborhood kids liked to come over and play at Kyonn's house. Kyonn lived with his mom and dad. His mom was a schoolteacher at a school for the blind. She was light-skinned, short, and had long, black hair that she always wore in hair ties.

His dad was over six feet tall, brown-skinned and very muscular. He was a firefighter for the Parkville Fire Department. Kyonn is also brown-skinned with short black locs on top and a fade on the sides. He is four foot eleven but thinks he is six feet tall when playing basketball with his dad. Kyonn didn't have any brothers or sisters, but he had a lot of cousins. His dad had eight siblings and all of them had children.

Meet Mya

Mya's house also had three floors and a basement—just about the same size as Kyonn's house. Mya lived with her mom and dad. She had one sibling, Mary, who was away at college. Mya was happy when her sister left because she got to move into "the big room."

Both of Mya's parents had black hair and brown eyes. Her mother's black hair was curly like Shirley Temple. Mya believed they were meant for one another because they enjoyed all the same things. Mya's mom was a stay-at-home mom. She always wore lounge clothes like long shirts and sweatpants but when they would go out, her mother knew how to dress up and look like a movie star.

Mya has black curly hair like her mom. She has brown skin and light brown eyes. She got her style from watching what her mother wore. Her dad was an accountant. He was always telling Mya she should save her allowance and put her money in the bank. Mya listened to her dad and has a nice savings account right now.

Meet Tycho

Tycho's house was the biggest. It had four bedrooms and three full bathrooms. It was a single-family home with three levels and an added family room for entertainment.

Tycho is the spitting image of his father. They both have dark hair, but Tycho's hair is spiky like a rock star, and they're both very fair-skinned. His dad is a photographer and film director. He often takes Tycho on movie sets with him.

Tycho's mom is a petite lady with short black hair and a mole on her right cheek. She always wore makeup since she was a teenager which inspired her to start her own company, Blush & Paint Makeup Studio.

Meet Sophia

Sophia's house was smaller, with only two floors and no basement. She was raised by her father, Kurt. She had three siblings including two sisters, Nicole and June, and one brother, Max. Sophia is the middle child. Her dad turned one of the first-floor rooms into his home office where he worked during the day as an architect. The office wasn't big—just a desk, computer, and drawers for papers and plans. Sophia enjoyed the stories her father would tell her about the buildings he had helped design. Sophia's dad had brown hair and a big brown beard. He was a hard worker and always tried his best to motivate Sophia in whatever she pursued.

The Crew

They all attended the same neighborhood school called Antluz Middle School. They were all sixth graders in Mrs. Ackromen's homeroom class. Tycho and Kyonn sat across from each other and would often sneak to text one another in class. Mrs. Ackromen kept a tight watch on her class so they couldn't play around like they normally did. Mya and Sophia also sat next to each other. They would whisper and write notes to one another whenever Mrs. Ackromen wasn't watching.

The Crew enjoyed being at school. They were especially looking forward to class on Monday. That was the day the principal, Mr. Greg, was going to make a huge announcement.

Chapter 2

THE ANNOUNCEMENT

Benjamin Lopez

There was a continuous buzz in the hallway. The students were all moving at once, seemingly heading nowhere. They were going up and down the hallway in every direction possible. There was no way to pass the crowd that was growing; it was crammed. Up and down the stairs, there were children everywhere.

"Hey Tycho," Kyonn spoke louder than normal over the buzzing voices. "You think we got the trip to Disney World?"

"Yeah, we definitely got the trip," replied Tycho, smiling, holding back his excitement.

The trip had to do with academic achievement, and the four friends were all about excelling in school.

"Sixth graders report to the auditorium," the intercom interrupted the buzzing conversations with Mr. Greg's voice.

The principal's announcement caused a new stir of movement.

In the hall, finally, their class was asked to line up in the same order as always which was Liv, Sophia, Mya, John, Jack, Malcolm, Kyonn, Tycho, and finally Zion. Mrs. Ackromen made sure everyone was in the line by calling their name. Their response, "Here," allowed them to continue in line and go into the auditorium. The excitement of the announcement had everyone smiling as they tried to be still.

"Mya, this is it! They're announcing how we earned a spot for the trip."

Sophia looked so happy. She'd been waiting so long. The announcement that one of the sixth-grade classes would win a trip had been made six months ago.

Kyonn questioned Tycho again. "Do you remember when they said we could earn a trip to Disney World?"

"Yes, I do." Tycho smiled at his friend.

Kyonn continued as they walked with their classmates down the hall. "And today they'll announce who got a spot on the bus. What are the chances we will go to Disney World?"

"One out of 5 or 20%," said Jack. Jack loved math.

"Those odds seem pretty good to me," said Kyonn. "If we win, I'm going on the safari ride."

"Nah, we should go in the theater with the water that sprays. That would be more fun than a safari ride," replied Jack. "I think the theater is funner."

"Funner is not a word, Jack." Kyonn shook his head as the group laughed.

The four friends—Kyonn, Mya, Sophia, and Tycho—found seats together in the auditorium. As Jack entered, he tripped and then slipped on a banana peel that fell out of his coat pocket from lunch. He grabbed the back of the auditorium chair before hitting the floor as if nothing happened. His classmates snickered, trying not to laugh aloud with the rest of the students in Mrs. Ackromen's class.

The attention turned to the stage. The students were waiting for Mr. Greg. He was a skinny man with dark blond hair. The students thought it looked like a bad dye job. Mr. Greg was about five feet, six inches tall. He was wearing a gold tuxedo jacket, and it had a little picture of Mickey Mouse on the pocket. He was also wearing gold pants.

Mr. Greg stood on the side of the stage holding a small gold envelope in his hand.

Once all the classes were seated and quiet, Mr. Greg stepped to the middle of the stage and began to speak. "Good afternoon students, I know you all are excited about the trip."

The students replied with loud applause and a buzz of whispers filled the room. Then they grew quiet, doing a great job of getting themselves under control and staying focused.

"Are you guys ready for me to announce the winner?" Mr. Greg asked, stirring the excitement again.

Everyone began yelling and hollering about which class would get picked.

Mr. Yolor's class was probably the biggest competition for Mrs. Ackromen's class. Mr. Yolor was very smart and had been teaching at the school for twenty-nine years. Mrs. Ackromen had been teaching for sixteen years, but she always had a smaller class. The competition between the teachers began when they were children. They were related, brother and sister, but had different last names because Mrs. Ackromen got married five years ago.

Mr. Greg walked across the stage slowly, overlooking the students who were sitting in anticipation. He walked to the middle of the stage and stopped in the center of the spotlight. He looked a bit nervous for some reason.

It was six months earlier when Mr. Greg came into Mrs. Ackromen's classroom around 9 a.m. He did what everyone thought was one of the strangest things in the world. He ran into the room wearing a Mickey Mouse hat, tail, and shirt. Everybody in the class thought he had lost it. The entire class was laughing their socks off. The laughter continued as the teachers stood before the students smiling. They couldn't stop laughing.

After about five minutes, Mr. Greg said, "Okay, okay, you've had a good laugh now it's time to pay attention."

It was hard to stop laughing. It was so funny. It took a moment, but everyone eventually became quiet.

Mr. Greg continued. "I have an announcement. A sixth-grade class will be chosen to go to Disney World at the end of the year."

The students' eyes widened with wonder and surprise. The chatter amongst classmates began instantly. Everyone in the classroom started whispering to each other.

John asked Malcolm, "You think it will be us?" Then he looked to Liv and said, "This is so exciting! It could be our class."

Liv answered without hesitation, "I have to go to Disney World; I've always wanted to go."

Jack said to Zion, "If we get chosen, it will be so much fun."

"Yeah, it will," said Zion.

Kyonn and Tycho sat in their own thoughts wondering if they could really earn the trip.

Sophia smiled and told Mya, "If we go, we're riding a rollercoaster."

"Ok, class, let's listen to Mr. Greg now," said Mrs. Ackromen.

"Like I was saying, you can earn a trip to Disney World in Orlando, Florida. There will be a day at Disney World and a dance with sixth and seventh graders from ten different schools from all over. Now if you want to go, you must work hard and get your class above 90% for the final overall grade. The class with the highest overall grade point average will go to Disney World. Since you have the smallest class in sixth grade with only nine students, it should be easier for you than the other classes. Okay, now that you know this, I'll let you go."

"Okay students, what do we say to Mr. Greg for taking his time to share this information with us?" Mrs. Ackromen asked the class.

"Thank you, Mr. Greg!" The students replied, filled with joy and happiness.

They all agreed to put in their best efforts. So, it became the goal to work as hard as they could to try to earn the trip to Disney World.

Now in the auditorium, they were about to unveil the winner. Before they announced the winner, Mr. Greg called Mrs. Jackson to the stage to say a few words. Mrs. Jackson, the seventh-grade teacher, came onstage and said, "I am proud of you all for your hard work. Even if your class is not chosen, there is another chance to win next year's trip. Keep working hard and congratulations to the winners. Okay, now Mr. Greg will announce the winner."

"Thank you, Mrs. Jackson," Mr. Greg said into the microphone as she stepped back. "The time has finally come. I am now opening the envelope to announce the winner."

The gold envelope seemed to glow with the little Mickey Mouse sticker seal on it, and the entire auditorium was silent as Mr. Greg opened it. Some people couldn't look, and there were others who crossed their fingers. Everyone in Mrs. Ackromen's class looked anxious as their hearts beat nervously.

Mr. Greg opened the envelope and announced, "The winner is…" The pause seemed to take forever. "Mrs. Ackromen's class with an overall grade average of 99%."

The yelling and hooting began as the students from Mrs. Ackromen's class shouted with joy. The other students responded with clapping.

Mrs. Ackromen stood up to get the class to be quiet as she whispered, "You have done very well. You can talk later, but right now, please listen to Mr. Greg."

"Wow, I cannot believe we are going to Disney World!" said Mya.

"I know! It's crazy we won. I knew we would, but I still can't believe it," said Sophia.

Mya replied, "But the ride will be so long. How many hours will it take? This is so exciting. Imagine what we'll see just riding to get there. The bus ride with all of us, girl, that will be crazy!"

Mr. Greg addressed the crowd. "Okay students, thank you for your hard work. Mrs. Ackromen, your class is to be congratulated. Thank you all for your participation. You are dismissed to go back to your classrooms."

Mr. Greg left the stage and Mrs. Ackromen gave the students instructions. "Please line up in order and don't forget to please be quiet in the hallway."

Last to leave the auditorium, the class exited and received congratulations from Mr. Yolor as they stood waiting in line. Everyone was whispering to each other about how they got a free trip to Disney World.

"I'm just so happy we won. Mr. Yolor's class was so close to beating us. I'm amazed. I thought they might have won, but we did, it's crazy. If Mr. Greg said it a hundred times over, I'd still be in disbelief," said Sophia.

"This is so cool. Just think about it. We get a free trip to Disney World in three weeks," said Tycho.

"I know, right. I knew it would be us. It was obvious. I knew it the whole time," replied Kyonn.

Malcolm thought about what Kyonn said. Maybe he was right. The class worked so hard it was impossible for them not to win.

Liv yelled, "Yes, yes, I'm so happy! This is so cool! I've always wanted to go to Disney World!"

Mrs. Ackromen's class filed into the classroom. Everyone was happy, including Mrs. Ackromen, who didn't get overjoyed easily. The class could not stop talking as if everyone had eaten a pound of cotton candy. The energy was off the charts. Mrs. Ackromen decided not to give the students any assignments as all they could talk about was winning the Disney World trip.

Instead, she handed out letters for each student to take home to their parents and said, "Class, this is very important so please listen carefully. I'm giving each of you a letter that has more information about the trip. For example, our bus will be leaving at 6:15 a.m. This is a twelve to fourteen-hour trip and we will be gone for one week. You must pack your own snacks for the bus. You should bring enough money for your expenses, enough to last the entire trip. And in this paperwork, we have provided a guide as to how much certain activities will cost.

We will make several stops on the journey to Orlando, Florida. We will also stop at the large mall while in Orlando. There will be a dance for all the winning schools to attend. You will be staying at the Happy Town Hotel while there. Your days will be filled with being at Disney World and enjoying the attractions. I'm sure you will have fun."

After the announcement, the class continued to do their schoolwork and other things to pass the time. They would try to contain their excitement and have a normal school week. There were only a few weeks left before they would leave. Until then, Mrs. Ackromen reminded the class of an important event the following week—science projects had to be completed for the science fair, and everyone was still required to participate and turn in their assignments before leaving.

When they got home, the students told their parents about the science fair.

Chapter 3

THE SCIENCE FAIR

Ann Taylor

There were only four students in Mrs. Ackromen's class that participated in the science fair—Tycho, Mya, Sophia, and Kyonn. They all met with Mrs. Ackromen, Mr. Mohammed the science teacher, and Mrs. Jackson the seventh-grade teacher after school in the science classroom. The classroom had white walls full of posters about the science fair. There was one science pun on the wall that made Sophia laugh. It read: "Why did the chemist read the book on helium so fast? He couldn't put it down." At the front of the classroom, there was a big projector and screen.

In the corner, behind the desk, was a box full of beakers and cardboard, syringes, plastic bags, and other things used for science experiments. There were three shelves on the wall. On the very top shelf there was a jar filled with some type of chemical that had all the colors of the rainbow.

Tycho, Mya, Sophia, and Kyonn helped Mrs. Jackson put the desks in a small circle, and they all sat down.

"Let's see what you guys already have," said Mrs. Jackson.

Tycho went first. He excitedly presented his project, saying, "I made chemicals!" While mixing them, he said, "When you mix these together, they make a mini explosion."

Mrs. Ackromen shouted, "Don't mix them together now!!" Right after she spoke, there was an explosion—a big boom that caused the foam from the chemicals to spread across the room, all over everything.

Tycho replied with a crooked smile, "Sorry about that."

After they cleaned the mess up, Mya proudly presented her project. "I made a model solar system!"

"This is very impressive, Mya!" Mrs. Jackson said, and the other teachers agreed.

You could tell that each planet was carefully made. The rings on Saturn were sparkly and it looked like the asteroids were floating in the air. The sun was glowing brightly. Everyone was impressed.

Kyonn said, "Wow, Mya! That's amazing!"

Next it was Sophia's turn, and she presented her model volcano.

"This is my wondrous volcano!" she said happily.

It was very detailed and looked very real. The base of the volcano was various shades of brown and black. It had green spots on it that looked like moss. Mrs. Ackromen felt the volcano and the texture was rough. There were little bumps and dents along the volcano, adding to the realistic effect.

Mr. Mohammed asked, "Don't you think a lot of other kids made a volcano?"

Sophia replied with a smirk, "This is no ordinary model volcano, it has imitation lava!"

Tycho was confused and asked, "What is imitation lava?"

"I'm glad you asked," Sophia said as she picked up some gloves, put them on, then picked up the liquid chemicals next to the volcano. "Imitation lava is my creation; it looks like real lava and is also extremely hot. The materials I used to make the volcano can withstand the heat, but if you touch the imitation lava, you will get burned."

"That's really cool!" Mya exclaimed. "Can we see?"

Mrs. Ackromen said anxiously, "I don't think that's a good idea. Let's do that somewhere outside of the classroom. In fact, it may be best if you save your volcano until the science fair."

Next up was Kyonn. "I made something that has never been made before! I call it Mannequin Robot!"

A wave of confusion fell over the room.

"What's a mannequin robot?" Sophia asked.

Kyonn smiled and said, "Let me show you."

He took a remote similar to a gaming controller out of the solid blue metal box next to him and pressed a button. The mannequin came to life and he moved it around with the toggles on the controller.

"Woah! That's so cool!" said the children.

Mrs. Ackromen, Mr. Mohammed, and Mrs. Jackson were also very impressed with what Kyonn made.

With the science fair deadline approaching, the kids worked hard to perfect their projects. They met up with their teachers every other day and were confident that their projects would win the competition.

* * *

When they all arrived at the Baltimore Convention Center, the science fair was a big event. In the middle of the room, they saw a solar system model just like Mya's. The walls of the room were like a galaxy and even had little stars and asteroids. The floor was covered in black carpet, but everyone was mesmerized by the solar system.

There were big stairs leading to the upper level, but the kids stayed at the bottom. The students and teachers went over to their tables. There was enough space to fit all of their projects. The teachers helped the kids unpack the projects onto the tables.

"The other kids sure have a lot of good stuff," Tycho said nervously.

Kyonn replied confidently, "Don't worry, I bet we'll win this thing. Our creations are the best!"

"Let's get ready everybody, the science fair is going to start in about ten minutes," Mrs. Ackromen said.

The kids got situated and stood in front of their projects. A woman came up to a podium in front of the big solar system in the center of the room.

"Welcome, everybody! Boys and girls, kids and teachers! Thank you for coming all the way here! My name is Ms. Honey, and I will be your host and judge!"

"She's really loud," Mya whispered to Sophia.

"Tell me about it," Sophia whispered back.

"But I will not be the only judge here," Ms. Honey continued, loudly. "There are two others, Mr. H. and Ms. Swan!"

Everyone watched as the two other judges walked up to the podium.

"We are so glad to be here today," said Mr. H. with a hint of sarcasm.

"We can't wait to see what you all have!" Ms. Swan said kindly.

After a few minutes, the judges began walking around the display tables.

Sophia, Kyonn, Tycho, and Mya all looked at each other very nervously.

"What if they don't like what we have?" Mya said frantically.

Kyonn tried to be the big one in the group and said, "Stop worrying, the judges will like our projects the most!"

But everyone could see that Kyonn was nervous too.

Mrs. Ackromen, Mrs. Jackson, and Mr. Mohammed cheered the students up by bringing some of their favorite snacks.

Once Ms. Honey, Mr. H., and Ms. Swan got to their table, Mya was first. She showed them the solar system. Ms. Honey, Mr. H., and Ms. Swan were impressed with the details and even applauded. Mya's confidence was boosted and a big smile spread across her face. Next up was Tycho. The judges looked at his beakers and chemicals.

"What are these?" Mr. H. asked.

"I made these chemicals from scratch and found a new way to make things explode," Tycho replied somewhat nervously.

Ms. Honey, Mr. H., and Ms. Swan looked at each other, impressed that he made the chemicals from scratch.

Ms. Swan asked, intrigued, "Could you show us?"

Tycho took a breath, mixed his chemicals together, and created an explosion. Foam flew all over the table. Mya, Sophia, and Kyonn stood in front of their projects to make sure they didn't get messed up or dirty.

"Incredible!" said Ms. Honey. The two other judges were also impressed.

Next was Sophia. She was nervous and a bit embarrassed because she was covered in foam but wiped it off and presented her project.

"This is my volcano!" Sophia said, trying to sound confident.

Ms. Honey, Mr. H., and Ms. Swan were unimpressed.

Mr. H. looked at Sophia and said, "You know, a lot of other kids made a volcano. What makes yours so special?"

Sophia looked at Mr. H. and said, "This volcano has something I made called imitation lava."

Ms. Honey was confused. "What is imitation lava?" she asked.

"Imitation lava is something I made. It looks like real lava and is very hot. The materials I use to make the volcano can withstand the heat of the imitation lava, but if you touch the lava, you will get burned," Sophia explained.

"Could you show us a demonstration of your volcano?" Ms. Honey asked.

"Sure," Sophia said nervously.

She put on the gloves that were nearby, picked up the chemicals, and started mixing them in the volcano. A few seconds later, the volcano started to erupt. Ms. Honey, Mr. H., and Ms. Swan looked very impressed. They approached the volcano to see the imitation lava in motion from a closer view and could feel the heat. Ms. Honey, Mr. H., and Ms. Swan were astonished that a sixth grader accomplished something like this.

They congratulated her and moved on to Kyonn. He was anxious because he was the last one and he thought he would be horrible, but he took a breath and stood up straight. Ms. Honey, Mr. H., and Ms. Swan walked over to him.

Kyonn showed them the mannequin. Ms. Honey, Mr. H., and Ms. Swan were a bit confused but trusted the process.

"This is a mannequin robot; I can make it move with a controller," Kyonn said as he picked up the controller from the table. He pressed the button in the middle and the mannequin came to life.

"Woah!" said Ms. Swan.

Kyonn used the controller to make the mannequin pose and dance. The judges' jaws dropped; they were so amazed.

Mr. H. shook Mr. Mohammed's hand and said, "I have very high hopes for your school."

After Ms. Honey, Mr. H., and Ms. Swan went to all of the tables, they went back to the podium.

"We will now announce the top three winners of this year's science fair!" Ms. Honey shouted.

"For third place we have Chiller Park Middle School," Mr. H. said loudly.

Everyone applauded as the kids and the teachers from Chiller Park ran up and got the trophy. The Chiller Park students were so happy. The judges presented the teachers of Chiller Park with a check for $100 for their school.

After the people from Chiller Park went back to their table, Ms. Swan called the next school.

"Second place for the science fair is…The Wellington School!"

Once again, applause filled the room. The kids and teachers went up to get the trophy and a check for $200, then they went back to their table. Everyone was anxiously waiting to hear the first-place winner announced. The lights dimmed and a spotlight shined on the podium.

"First place for the yearly science fair is Antluz Middle School!" Ms. Honey yelled.

Mya, Sophia, Tycho, and Kyonn all cheered and hugged each other as they went up to the podium with Mr. Mohammed and Mrs. Jackson to get the trophy. Ms. Honey presented Mr. Mohammed with a check for $500 for Antluz Middle School. Mya, Sophia, Tycho, and Kyonn were so happy as they held the trophy together. They all felt very accomplished.

Chapter 4
THE JOURNEY

Dylan Turner

It was 5:30 a.m. and it was still dark outside, but the sun was beginning to rise when Kyonn's mother pulled into the school parking lot. She turned off the car and walked around to Kyonn's side to open the door.

"Ok, son, we are here."

His mother leaned into the car only to find that Kyonn had dozed off during the short ride from their home.

Kyonn got out of the car and began stretching. Letting his arms drop and shaking off the morning drowsiness, he grabbed his duffle bag that sat beside him.

"I'm going to miss your silly self," Kyonn's mother said as she gave him a loving hug. "Now have fun, but don't get in any trouble. Do you have your cell phone?"

"Yes, Ma," Kyonn answered.

"Do you have your Cash App card and the cash I gave you?" his mother asked, continuing down her list of questions.

They were the same questions she asked each time Kyonn went on any trip.

"Yes, Ma," Kyonn responded with an annoyed sigh.

Then he looked at her with his head tilted to the side, letting her know he was ready to be on his journey. She gave him one last hug then got back in her car. She rode off slowly watching her son walk into the school lobby.

The class was told it would be a long trip to Disney World—twelve to fifteen hours to Florida. As Kyonn passed the oversized black and white bus provided by Disney World he thought, Boy it's going to be a BORING ride.

"Wow, that bus…like wow. It can hold about fifty people!" said Tycho.

Mr. Bushmen, the bus driver, was standing in front of the school entrance greeting everyone as they walked into the lobby. He had on what the children called "really wack clothes"—big black shoes and baggy pants that had patterns like a clown's costume. His shirt had a spinning fidget bow tie. They wondered if he had another job as a clown.

Everyone was directed to line up in the school lobby like little kids. Mrs. Cloud, the assistant for Mrs. Ackromen's class whipped out her handy clipboard with everyone's name on it and started a head count of all the students.

"Ok, listen up, everyone. I'm going to call your name and when I do, walk over to the bus and Mrs. Jackson will ask you your name again. Then you can board the bus... understand?"

Mrs. Cloud stood tapping her pen on the clipboard waiting for a response. Everyone just looked at her; no one said anything.

Her face was getting red and she repeated, "UNDERSTAND!?"

The students knew what her tone meant so they all said "Yes" at the same time as though they were in a choir.

"Liv Heartlock, John Johnson, Zion Miller."

Mrs. Cloud was calling the names for everyone to walk to the bus. Kyonn was hoping he wouldn't be called last because he wanted to pick his own seat next to the window.

Finally, Mrs. Cloud yelled out, "Kyonn Snacks."

Kyonn, walking with a little bop, bumped against his best friend Tycho and whispered, "Yo, I'mma save you a seat."

Tycho and Kyonn bumped fists, exchanged a smile, and Tycho said, "Good looking out."

Kyonn didn't walk to the bus, he was moving so fast he was walk-running. Finally, he reached the bus and Mrs. Jackson asked, "Your name?"

Kyonn gave her a peculiar look, but he didn't question her and answered, "Kyonn Snacks."

Everyone ran to find seats next to their friends. Kyonn and Tycho ran to sit together, and so did Sophia and Mya. The group sat across from each other. When the other students Liv, John, Malcom, Jack, and Zion got on the tour bus they were really hyped. The students agreed the bus was hooked up. It wasn't a regular bus. Everything to occupy their time was available. It had a huge bathroom, sleeping pods, and there were eight or more televisions. There were two Xbox Series S's, two Nintendos, and two PS5's. It was a fantasy come true.

It was 6:15 am and the bus began to move. Malcolm just randomly started singing the Little Einsteins theme song and everyone started to mimic him. After singing it close to twenty-five times, the lyrics transitioned into chatter about the trip. Liv and Malcolm were talking about how long the trip would be and how many stops they would make. Tycho, Mya, and Sophia were talking about how their hotel would look. As the conversation was ending, Tycho turned around to see Kyonn had dozed off.

Kyonn was awake all night long packing and didn't get any sleep. The letter Mr. Greg sent home with all the students said to pack a bag because the trip would be a week long. Kyonn knew he was going to be sleeping on and off on the bus ride, so he packed A LOT. It was like he had his whole bedroom in one duffle bag. With his neck pillow, he fell right to sleep.

"Dang, he's snoring LOUD!" said Tycho.

One hour and twenty minutes later, they were passing the Washington Monument located at the National Mall in Washington, D.C. Everyone, except Kyonn who was still asleep, enjoyed the view.

At 8 a.m. Mrs. Ackromen stood up to announce they would be handing out bags with breakfast items to everyone. She made it a point to say only one bag per person because Tycho loved to eat. He could eat three breakfasts if they let him.

Kyonn finally woke up while Mrs. Ackromen was speaking. Tycho told Kyonn he missed the ride past the Washington Monument and the museum. Tycho was excited to share some facts he had learned about the monument and explained, "The Washington Monument survived an earthquake. It took almost forty years to complete its construction. It's two different shades of white because construction had stopped for two decades and ultimately took place in two phases, so the quarry stone couldn't be matched."

Kyonn looked at him and said, "Did you read about this?"

Tycho said, "Yep, and also in the Virginia Museum of Fine Arts some of Kehinde Wiley's artwork is on display."

"Who is that?" asked Kyonn.

"Kehinde Wiley is the artist that made President Obama's portrait in the White House," answered Malcolm.

The friends started to eat their packaged breakfast: one apple, a muffin, a fruit cup, and a juice box.

After the so-called breakfast, the teachers collected the trash from everyone. It was very quiet on the bus. Kyonn looked around and noticed that everyone had fallen asleep. He needed to use the bathroom but didn't want to wake anyone, so he moved very quietly to the restroom. Then he came back, put on his headphones, hopped on the PS5, and played for hours.

The bus driver announced they would be making their first stop in Raleigh, North Carolina. It took Mr. Bushmen a little over five hours to arrive in Raleigh. Mrs. Jackson stood up to say that they would be visiting Pullen Park. She asked if anyone knew anything about Pullen Park and there was dead silence.

She then said, "Well, Pullen Park is one of the oldest parks in the world and it has lots of fun things you can do. The park has a community center, a playground, an aquatic center, a theater, and a whole bunch more. But we decided that we would stop at the aquatic center for some fun."

The students played in Pullen Park for over an hour before Mrs. Jackson came to gather everyone for lunch at the Pullen Café. The café was small but had unique items on the walls. The students and teachers were escorted to a private section in the back of the café. The students sat and chatted with one another until lunch was served.

After an hour, they went back on the tour bus and rode for another four hours.

Kyonn couldn't help himself and went back to sleep until they arrived at Myrtle Beach, South Carolina. They drove past the Hollywood Wax Museum and stopped at Hannah's Maze of Mirrors. The students thought it was cool. They also went to Outbreak: Dread the Undead which gave all of them a good scare.

Mr. Bushmen would make a couple more rest stops before arriving at the Happy Town Hotel on the Disney property in Florida.

Chapter 5

MAGICAL DAY

Benjamin Lopez, Ann Taylor,
Dylan Turner, Kaylani Turner

In the heart of spring with the sun shining brightly and a summertime breeze, the students buzzed with anticipation. The teachers had been planning a trip to Disney World for months and finally, the day had arrived. After a long bus ride from Baltimore to Orlando, the teachers and students were ready to have some serious fun.

In the courtyard of the hotel, amidst a flurry of enthusiasm and chatter, the friends gathered around, deciding on which rollercoaster they were most eager to ride and strategizing the best way to see all the attractions. Malcolm, the planner of the group, held a map of the Hollywood Studios Park in his hands as his eyes gleamed with excitement.

"Okay, everyone," he announced, drawing the attention of his friends, "we need to have a game plan. We want to make the most of every second at the park!"

The group—Liv, John, Jack, Zion, Mya, Sophia, Kyonn, Tycho, and Malcolm—huddled together, discussing their plans. Jack, Zion, and Sophia were eager to rush straight to the tallest rollercoaster, while the others couldn't wait to get on the stomach-churning drop tower. Amidst the laughter and chitchat, they mapped out their day, making sure to include time for snacks.

As they boarded the bus, the excitement became more evident. The students told stories of past adventures at an amusement park and shared tips on how to beat the longest lines. The bus ride passed in a blur of laughter and anticipation, the minutes ticking away until they reached their destination.

"Welcome to Disney World!" exclaimed Mrs. Ackromen, her voice brimming with anticipation. "Today is all about fun."

The sight of the towering rollercoasters and colorful attractions left them breathless. With a collective cheer, they poured out of the bus and into the park, ready to seize the day.

Their first stop was the iconic Slinky Dog Dash, a family-friendly rollercoaster that takes riders on a fun-filled journey through Andy's backyard aboard Slinky Dog. Mrs. Jackson took some of the children on the Slinky Dog Dash and others went to see the Beauty and the Beast show. With their hearts pounding and adrenaline racing, they were all laughing, holding their chests, and talking about their favorite part of the ride.

Throughout the day, they raced from one ride to the next, their laughter mingling with the sounds and distant screams. They conquered towering ferris wheels and dizzying spinning rides. Amidst the thrill rides and immersive experiences, the students also took the time to appreciate the art of storytelling. They attended workshops where they learned about animation, special effects, and character design. And they gained a deeper understanding of the creative process behind their favorite films.

As the sun began to go down, the students gathered for one final thrill. With a sense of accomplishment, they joined hands and braved the tallest, fastest rollercoaster in the park, screaming with exhilaration as they soared through the air. As they stumbled off the ride, hearts racing and cheeks flushed with excitement, they exchanged high fives and hugs, and their faces lit up with joy.

"We did it!" Jack said, his voice filled with pride. "We conquered every ride in Disney World!"

With memories of a day filled with laughter, adventure, and friendship, they boarded the bus back to the hotel, planning the next day. For these students, the trip to the amusement park had been more than just a day of fun—it had been an unforgettable journey filled with excitement and shared moments they would treasure forever.

Chapter 6

THE DANCE

Kaylani Turner

Mya let out a big sigh.

"Ughh … I don't know which dress to wear," she said as she looked at her two outfit options on the bed.

It was a week ago on a Saturday afternoon when Mya and her best friend, Sophia, were dropped off by Mya's mom at the Antluz Mall which was located down the street from their school.

The mall, which looked as big as a mansion, was a popular place that was always crowded on Saturdays because the cool kids hung out there. It had four levels which included tons of stores and a huge eatery. Every time they were able to visit the mall, Mya and Sophia always made a stop to get their favorite smoothie from a spot called Five Star Smoothies. Sophia always ordered the strawberry-banana smoothie, but Mya loved the mango green tea drinks.

They had their choice of stores to visit but didn't get very far because while traveling up the escalator within minutes of their arrival, Mya spotted a gorgeous dress through the glass window of the store Taylor Designs.

"That is my dress!" she exclaimed. "It is perfect!"

Sitting there looking back at them was a sparkly black dress with short sleeves.

Sophia said, "Come on let's go in; I bet I can find one too!"

Just then Mya's phone rang. It was her mom asking her if everything was ok.

Mya responded, "Yea, everything is fine; I will call you back."

Her response came off a little short and you could hear the irritation in her voice, but she really did not mean any harm. Mya loved her mom, but she felt she was a bit overprotective.

As they entered the store, Mya could not keep her eyes off the dress. It was obvious that her mind was already made up about it. Sophia, on the other hand, felt like she would need some help finding a dress that would complement her since she was one who would always come to school dressed in ripped jeans and a crop top sweater along with her favorite Converse tennis shoes. She loved them so much that she happened to have them in every flavor imaginable.

As Sophia continued to look around the store, a salesperson named Jasmin asked her if she needed help. Sophia responded, "Yes, please."

She told Jasmin that she was looking for a plain red dress that had short sleeves for her school dance. She explained that she was not into girly clothing.

Jasmin chuckled and said, "I understand. I was the same when I was your age."

Jasmin did not waste any time finding Sophia the exact dress she had described. At that moment, Mya appeared and asked Jasmin if she could try on the black sparkly, short-sleeved dress in the window. Mya and Sophia both went into the dressing room area to see how their dresses fit. They ended up being in dressing rooms that were next to each other.

Mya yelled, "How does your dress fit Sophia?"

Sophia responded, "Good, how about yours?"

Mya said, "Good. Let's show each other our dresses," and Sophia swiftly agreed.

They both came out of their dressing rooms simultaneously.

Sophia exclaimed, "I love your dress! It makes you look like a supermodel."

Sophia already expected Mya to look nice because she is the type of girl that always liked to match her outfits and dress nicely.

Mya then said, "Thank you," and agreed that Sophia's dress was her type of style as well.

Jasmin came over and said, "You guys look pretty. Should I wrap those dresses up for you?"

Both girls said "Yes" and used their Cash App cards to pay for them.

After checking them out, Jasmin handed them their bags and said, "Have a great time at your dance, ladies!"

Mya then called her mom.

"Mom, we found our dresses and are ready to go."

Her mom replied, "Ok, meet me in front of the bookstore."

On their way to the bookstore, Mya and Sophia walked by a store called Best Dresses in Town where Mya spotted another pretty dress that was pink and sparkly. It had thin straps and white gloves that came with it.

Mya said, "This dress is also very pretty; let's go inside."

She began searching on the dress rack for a size medium. Once she found one, she held it up and asked, "Sophia, should I get it?"

Sophia replied, "Do you have enough on your Cash App card for two dresses?"

Mya responded, "Yes, my mom gave me some extra money for the dance."

Sophia shook her head as Mya went to the cash register to pay for her second dress.

On the car ride home, Mya's mother, Mrs. Johnson, dropped Sophia off at her house, which was a block away from Mya's. As they headed home, Mrs. Johnson asked Mya to put on a fashion show and show off her two new dresses. Once they arrived home, Mya ran to her bedroom and tried on her first dress, the one she called the "black sparkling dress." She went downstairs where her mother and father were sitting patiently in the living room.

Mya's dad said, "Mya, that is a very nice dress."

Her mom could not contain herself and with tears falling from her eyes she said, "Wow, you look beautiful in that dress."

Mya then ran back upstairs to try on the pink dress and received similar responses from her parents.

Afterwards, Mya's mother asked her, "Which dress are you going to wear to the dance?"

Mya responded, "Honestly, I can't decide between the two. For now, I'll just plan to take them both with me to the hotel and make my decision at that time."

The Day of the Dance

Mya knows that she must decide on one of the dresses, and it has to be fabulous to wear to the dance in Disney World. In fact, she will need to do so immediately because she hears Mrs. Ackromen in the hallway outside of her hotel room knocking on doors alerting all the attendees that it's time to go. She finally decides to wear the pink dress with the straps because it reminds her of a dress she saw her mom wear in one of her high school photos. Mya put on her dress and accessories, then proceeded to put the black sparkly dress back in her suitcase so that it would not get damaged.

She thought, Maybe I'll get to wear it to another event someday soon.

Then, there was a knock on the door. Sophia opened it and Mrs. Ackromen said, "Come on ladies it is time to go. We must meet everyone in the lobby to board the bus to the school dance."

Sophia and Mya grabbed their small pocketbooks and headed down the hallway with the other young ladies behind Mrs. Ackromen. They could see the boys walking down the opposite hall with Mr. Mohammed.

Everybody then got on the bus.

Most of them were saying things like "Your outfit is nice." But there were a few pranksters who were in a huddle on the back of the bus whispering and laughing hysterically about how Sophia looked awkward in a dress and heels compared to how she usually dresses. They weren't being nice at all. Instead of admiring and complimenting her on how beautiful she looked, they were teasing about how she had been struggling to walk in heels on the way to the bus.

Thankfully she couldn't hear everything they were saying since she was seated several rows in front of them; however, she did notice them pointing at her and laughing.

Now, not only was she feeling subconscious about how she looked, but she also started feeling a little sad and discouraged about having to wear her outfit and possibly having to deal with further teasing for the next few hours. She decided it was best for her to turn around in her seat, insert her earphones into her ears, and listen to some good music to distract herself from their antics for the remainder of the bus ride.

Once they reached their destination—Treeville Middle School—Mya and Sophia saw how huge the school was. It was even bigger than the mansion-sized mall they had visited this week. Mya acknowledged that it was quite different from their school, which was much smaller.

When they entered the venue, they heard DJ Loud House say over the speakers, "Come on in the gym so we can get this party started."

With excitement, they started to head down to the gym. DJ Loud House put on the first song, and everyone loved it.

After a few songs, Sophia told Mya, "Hold on. I must take this phone call. I'll be back."

Sophia began walking down the hall. She wasn't sure where she was going but she realized that this phone call had to wait because she had to find the bathroom very fast.

She put the phone to her ear and stated, "Mom, we are here but I really need to find the bathroom. I will call you back."

Sophia hung up the phone and looked for a sign that said bathroom. At this point, she didn't care if it was a girls' or boys' bathroom.

She noticed a colorful light coming from underneath one of the closed doors. There was a sign on the door that read "Janitor's Closet." The light reminded her of a rainbow solution she saw in Mr. Mohammed's lab. She became distracted, forgot all about having to use the bathroom badly, and walked up to the door while still looking down at the rainbow light. She wanted to open the door, but should she?

* * *

It had been twenty minutes since Sophia left the dance and separated from the group. Mya had already made a new friend whose name was Sarah. Sarah was a sixth grader at Treeville Middle School. Sarah and Mya were doing all kinds of dances together, including the floss. After the song switched, the colors on the dance floor did too.

Mya reached over and asked Sarah, "Who is that strange man that keeps looking at us through the gym doors?"

Sarah replied, "Oh, that's Mr. Chuck, the school janitor."

Just then another sixth-grade class came into the gymnasium. One person was dressed in a costume and everyone was laughing at him, but he did not care one bit. He continued dancing his life away. Everyone was enjoying the experience.

Unfortunately, as everyone was having an enjoyable time, a fight between two of the students started because of a roast battle. They had been criticizing and making fun of each other's outfits, hair, shoes, family situations, grades in school, etc. for at least ten minutes. At first, it was all fun and games, but then the comments became heated and they began fighting.

The chaperones began running toward the crowd to break it up. Both students ended up being verbally reprimanded and were forced to sit in opposite corners of the gym. Once all the commotion died down, Mya abruptly remembered that Sophia had still not returned.

All the students except for Mya and Zion were doing silly dances. The chaperones were looking and laughing at the wonderful time everyone was having. That is when Mya told Kyonn and Tycho that Sophia had left to take a phone call but had been gone for a long time.

Tycho asked, "You let her go by herself?"

Mya said, "Well, she left to take a phone call."

Kyonn said, "Let's just go look for her."

Mya and Tycho said, "Ok. Let's go!"

Chapter 7

THE HUNT

Benjamin Lopez, Ann Taylor,
Dylan Turner, Kaylani Turner

Sophia kept being drawn to the light flickering under the door. She wanted to open it so badly, but she didn't know if that was a good idea. But her curiosity was stronger than her skepticism, so she cautiously pressed her ear up against the door attempting to hear if there was anything weird going on. At first, she hesitated to open the door but ended up doing so because she was determined to see what was behind it and what was causing that strange light.

Once she opened the door, her widened eyes moved around what turned out to be a big closet with brooms, mops, and other cleaning materials. Her trembling hand flew up and covered her mouth to stifle a gasp. She stared, in horror, as she witnessed Mr. Chuck, the janitor, transforming into an alien. In her state of shock, Sophia could still faintly hear the music from the party back in the main part of the gym.

Terrified, she tried to close the door quickly but, with lightning speed, Mr. Chuck's long alien arm slithered across the room and closed the door. Sophia turned and pulled on the doorknob while banging and screaming for help, but it was no use. She was locked inside the broom closet with no way to escape.

She turned around slowly, her insides shaking like a fluttering leaf. Mr. Chuck was a very scary person to look at. He was bald but had a big white beard. He had a humpback and was known to be a weird person.

Sophia was so scared. As she was about to scream again, she was put into a trance by some sort of dust he blew in her face that smelled like rotten eggs. When she came to, minutes later, Mr. Chuck had tied her up and she was bound to a chair. He was no longer in his alien form.

He stood there staring at her, looking normal, but she knew what she saw. And now, more than any time in her life, she had to use the bathroom; her insides rumbled and churned from nerves and shock. He walked around her chair like he was inspecting her.

She was scared out of her mind, but she had to ask him, "Wh-what are you? Where did you come from?"

"That's none of your concern," he said, in his old, raspy voice. "And let me warn you, there is no point in screaming because the room is soundproof."

Sophia started rocking back and forth in the chair. "Let me out of here you freaky alien. Let me go right now!"

She kept yelling and shouting for him to let her go but Mr. Chuck would not.

The scary janitor then hit a button on the wall and the room seemed to magically change. Sophia's eyes fell upon shelves and tables filled with different potions. She was very confused about what was happening. Mr. Chuck picked up his phone and proceeded to call someone.

Sophia overheard him talking. "Yeah, I got one of these students. Uh huh. She's a girl. Yes, I think we're almost ready."

Sophia couldn't understand what the person on the other end of the line was saying. After Mr. Chuck hung up the phone, she started asking a stream of questions.

"What is going on? Why am I here and what do you plan to do? You better let me go right now."

"Full of questions, eh? Sure, I'll tell you. We need test subjects to do some research to make sure it is safe."

At this point, Sophia was absolutely horrified and knew she had to find a way out of the janitor's broom closet that turned out to be some lab used for horrible experiments. Whatever "it" was, she didn't want to stick around to find out.

After a while, Mr. Chuck left. While he was gone, she tried to escape by pulling on the doorknob and using whatever she could find to try to open the lock, which wasn't much. Then, she yelled and screamed until her voice was hoarse and she realized that her cries for help were useless.

Meanwhile, back in the gym, Mya started asking their friends—Liv, Malcolm, Jack, and John—"Did you see Sophia? She went to take a phone call and didn't come back."

Tycho asked Mya and Kyonn, "Should I tell Mrs. Ackromen, or should we investigate?"

Jack asked, "Should we just leave Sophia?"

They all started laughing.

Mya spoke up and said, "Y'all not leaving my best friend."

Kyonn joined in and shouted, "No, seriously, if one of you went missing, how would y'all react? Wouldn't you want us to wait for you?"

In response, Liv questioned, "Are we going to look for Sophia or tell Mrs. Ackromen?"

"No, let's look for her because Mrs. Ackromen might cancel the dance," answered Mya.

Kyonn made the final decision when he said, "Let's start by looking by the bathrooms. Maybe that's where she was headed."

Tycho agreed. "Alright let's go, and don't tell anyone else."

Mya instructed Liv to be the lookout and to call her if Mrs. Ackromen or anyone else asked where they were.

The four friends started walking down the hallway, pulling on all the classroom door handles. No luck. They were all locked.

Kyonn said, "Hey, let's go downstairs and see if any of those doors are unlocked."

The others followed him down to the basement level. The lights were not bright like the lights on the upper level, but they could see where they were going. In soft whispery voices, they started calling Sophia's name hoping she would hear them and respond.

As they approached the end of the hallway, Tycho noticed the rainbow light coming from beneath the bottom of a door.

He whispered to the group, "Hey, hey." Drawing their attention, he said, "Look!" while pointing to the bottom of the door.

They all gathered in front of the door, and it was Tycho who turned the knob.

To their surprise, the door opened. At first it looked like a janitor's broom closet, but then Mya startled them once again when she said, "Look over there."

They took only a few steps inside the closet when they saw a big lab.

"What is this place?" Kyonn wondered.

Tycho chimed in and said, "It's like Doc Ock's lab from Spider-Man."

On the right side of the room were a lot of chemical beakers on shelves, animals in test tubes, and a computer with all the students' pictures who were at the dance.

Suddenly Mya yelled, "Sophia!"

Kyonn and Tycho turned around to see Sophia lying on a table with her eyes shut and wires going from her head to a bag above it. Hysterically, Mya yelled for them to disconnect the wires. Immediately, everyone started to pull the wires off Sophia's head. Mya began to shake Sophia and repeatedly called her name.

In distress she said to the others, "She's not waking up, what's wrong with her?"

Tycho moved over to assist Mya and gave Sophia a gentle slap on the face. Sophia opened her eyes, but she did not immediately recognize her friends.

Mya said, "Come on, let's get out of here."

Tycho's eyes came to rest upon a glowing light in a huge jar on the shelf.

He stated, "This is the same stuff in Mr. Mohammed's lab at school."

He then climbed up on a step ladder to pick up the jar. It fell out of his hand in what seemed like slow motion. There were shocked looks on everyone's faces as they were sure that the jar was going to hit the floor, but Kyonn caught the container before it shattered.

Mya looked at them while sighing with relief and said, "You both have slippery hands, give it to me."

Kyonn did not want to let the jar go. As the two played tug of war, the jar slipped between both of their hands and crashed to the floor.

Mya yelled at Kyonn, "See it's all your fault."

As Kyonn was about to yell back, they noticed the chemicals that had spilled from the jar gathering into four balls.

"Man, that's weird," said Tycho.

Before they could say anything else, the chemicals became attached to each of their legs.

Kyonn yelled, "Get it off me!" as he grabbed his leg, expecting to pull something off, but nothing visible was there.

None of them could see the chemicals that were just attached to their bodies, but each of them started to feel little shocks. Afraid that they were about to become entrapped, they held Sophia by the arms and ran out of the janitor's broom closet, up the stairs, and back to the dance.

Mya, Sophia, Kyonn, and Tycho walked into the gymnasium together. Tycho was still holding Sophia's arm because she was still weak and walking like she might fall at any moment. They sat down in four empty chairs alongside the wall.

Kyonn was still in shock and asked no one in particular, "What just happened?"

They looked at Sophia as if she could give them an explanation.

Mya asked, "Sophia, what happened to you?"

All Sophia could get out was, "He's an alien."

Unsure that they heard Sophia correctly, Tycho asked, "What did you say?"

Sophia looked at him and repeated, "The janitor is an alien. I saw the same light we saw in Mr. Mohammed's lab coming from under the door, so I opened it. I saw Mr.

Chuck turn into an ugly alien. He used his long arm to close the door. Then he tied me up. He put these wires on my head and pushed a button, then I started to feel sleepy."

The other students were still dancing and chatting with one another. At first everyone seemed to be having a great time, but then Mya started looking closely at some of them and they seemed to be moving slow just like Sophia.

She tapped Kyonn and said, "You see the girl over there in the yellow dress? Does she look like she is acting like Sophia?"

As Kyonn was checking out the girl in the yellow dress, Mya spotted a boy who was also moving slow like Sophia.

"There's another one. Do you see that? The same thing is wrong with them!"

Before Kyonn could answer, the principal of Treeville Middle School picked up the microphone and said, "Tonight has been a great night. I do hope everyone enjoyed themselves here at the Disney World Wonderland Dance. Please follow the directions of your teachers and safe travels."

Then the gym lights were turned up brightly. They remained seated until finally Mrs. Jackson called for Antluz Middle School to line up.

Liv saw the crew sitting down and ran over to ask, "Sophia, are you ok? We thought you were lost."

Mya, knowing Sophia was not herself, jumped in and said, "Yes, she is fine, just something she ate."

Satisfied with Mya's explanation, Liv said, "Ok, well, we better get in line before Mrs. Jackson blows a gasket."

Mya knew that Liv was correct, and if they didn't hurry up and get in line, Mrs. Jackson would pick up that something was wrong. They helped Sophia up and walked slowly to the back of the line to board the bus to the hotel.

The bus ride back to the hotel was quiet.

Sophia noticed that Mya, who was sitting beside her, kept blinking. She asked her, "Is something wrong with your eyes, Mya?"

Mya, not sure what was happening, rubbed her eyes and replied, "No, something must have flown into them."

Tycho turned around in his seat and whispered "Hey, let's meet at your room to talk about what happened. I still don't understand."

Mya nodded her head and said, "Ok, come to my room when the coast is clear."

The Happy Town Hotel was a small hotel on Disney property. The students from Antluz Middle School were all on the sixth floor. The rooms were very spacious with a sofa and a refrigerator.

About twenty minutes after getting back to the hotel room, Kyonn texted Mya to say, "We are on our way to your room."

Mya texted back, "Ok, I will open the door."

Mya got up from the sofa and gently opened her room door. She peeked her head out to see if she could see anyone and saw Kyonn and Tycho tiptoeing down the hallway. Once they reached Mya's room, she opened the door to let them in.

Tycho, not wasting any time getting back to the issue at hand, said, "This has been a crazy night. Word. Seriously, Sophia, aliens?"

Sophia sat up on the sofa and once again told them how she was captured.

"When I was on the table, I asked him why he was doing this, and he said that the aliens are trying to take the minds of young people to rejuvenate their species. I swear I'm not making this up."

Kyonn put his head in his hands as he shook in disbelief. "I still don't believe it. I mean, when I saw you on the table hooked up to those wires and all, I thought it was some crazy scientist but an alien?"

Mya jumped into the conversation, saying, "I think it may be true. Something is happening. I can feel something weird going on with my body ever since that stuff got on me."

Kyonn asked, "Weird like what?"

Mya paused then continued, "I've been seeing things. I can see things we did yesterday like they just happened, and I can see what's about to happen in the future. I can even see things that are happening right now, even if they are far away."

While looking at her friends, she saw that they were staring at her like she was crazy, but their faces changed when she began to show her power. Their mouths fell open when they saw a bright blue light flash in her right pupil as her iris widened. She stared straight ahead as if in a trance.

"When I open my eyes, I can see the present. When I close them, I can see the past and the future. Right now, I can see Mrs. Jackson is sleeping in her bed. Mr. Bushmen is in his bed too, even though he is awake and still has the TV on." Then, she turned toward Tycho and closed her eyes. "I can see into the past, when you received your special powers."

Tycho jumped up from his seat and asked with a squeal in his voice, "Who, me?"

Mya opened her eyes and said, "Yes, all of us received powers at the same time. There was a strange orange glow in the sky and then it slowly came down like smoke and surrounded us, but only I could see it. I didn't want to say anything in case I was bugging, but now I know that it's real."

She looked at Kyonn and said, "You can have great strength and climb tall buildings, and …"

Before Mya could finish, Sophia said, "She is right. All of a sudden, I can hear people talking far away and I can understand them talking in different languages, even Spanish, and that wasn't one of my best subjects. I didn't say anything because I thought no one would believe me."

Kyonn said, "Hold up. I can jump onto a building? Like from the street?"

Tycho, feeling left out, asked Mya, "Wait…what about me? What can I do?"

Mya replied, "I see you are energized with electricity powers. Let's go outside and try to test these powers just so I can be sure I'm not bugging out."

The crew agreed to sneak out of the hotel.

Kyonn, who could always find a way to get out of a building without being detected, found an exit door that would not let off any sirens. The door led them to the back of the hotel where the garbage bins were.

Kyonn walked up to Mya and said, "So you think I can jump on this building?"

Mya replied, "Yes. You may have to run then jump, but yes."

Kyonn was a confident person so at that moment he really believed he could do it. He jogged back to give himself some running space and then sprinted toward the building. Mya was standing there biting her nails as if to say, Boy I hope this works. Kyonn came flying by them and just before he leaped off the ground, his feet began to glow bright orange. He sprinted high up into the air and landed on the roof of the hotel. The hotel was only six stories high, but he made it.

Mya, Sophia, and Tycho were screaming with excitement to see their friend on the top of the building.

"Guys, be quiet, we are going to get in trouble if you keep screaming," Mya said to her friends.

"Me next, me next!" Tycho yelled. Then he turned to Mya and asked, "How can I use my electrical powers?"

Mya said to him, "You can lift things with a lightning bolt. And if you really focus, you can bend and heat things up. But whatever you do, don't hit any power lines. All you have to do is look at something and focus, then you can strike it with lightning or use a bolt to move it." Mya continued, "You control electricity, lighting, heating, and cooling."

Tycho was in deep thought trying to figure out how to use his power. He still seemed confused but turned to a small tree. Focusing only on the tree, he stretched both of his arms out and opened his hands toward it. Small veins of electricity began to travel down his arms to his hands and surrounded his fingers like rings. The tips of his fingers were ablaze. Suddenly, a flash of light flew from his hands and hit the tree. It split in half, falling to the ground. Another big round of shouting exploded from the crew.

"Shhhh," said Sophia.

Just then Mya saw someone open their room curtains.

"We better get back to the room before we get in trouble."

"We really do have superpowers," said Kyonn as he jumped down from the roof.

Mya replied, "Yeah, but what do we do with them?"

Kyonn looked at Mya and said, "First, we need to make a pact that no one else will learn about our powers. Second, we are going to use them to crush Mr. Chuck."

Chapter 8

THE PLAN

Benjamin Lopez, Ann Taylor,
Dylan Turner, Kaylani Turner

Mya, Sophia, Tycho, and Kyonn quietly walked into the hotel, took the elevator up to Sophia and Mya's floor, and used a key to enter their room.

"Everyone is sleeping," Sophia said. "I can hear them snoring in their rooms. We have to be quick before someone wakes up and knocks on our door to make sure we are sleeping."

"What about Mr. Chuck?" Tycho asked.

Sophia closed her eyes and focused hard on Mr. Chuck. She was quiet for a while.

Tycho was tired of waiting and yelled, "Hello! Sophia! Can you hear me?"

Kyonn loudly shushed Tycho, and Mya frowned at him. After another minute,

Sophia opened her eyes and sighed.

Mya asked curiously, "What did you hear?"

Kyonn and Tycho also wanted to know what Sophia heard.

"I didn't hear any talking," Sophia said with a disappointed look on her face. "It's night. Mr. Chuck and everyone else is asleep. I can hear him making noises. It doesn't sound like snoring, but he is making weird ticking noises."

"I can definitely see that he is sleeping," said Mya.

"It's fine, we can try again in the morning," Tycho said.

Kyonn, Mya, and Sophia agreed.

The crew knew they would be heading back to Baltimore soon and they only had one chance to destroy the alien before leaving Florida. Mya stood up from the sofa and closed her eyes; Kyonn looked at Sophia.

"Is she sleepwalking?" Kyonn asked Sophia.

"No silly," said Mya with her eyes still closed. "I can see a crowd of people on the football field behind the school. They have a band and cheerleaders." Mya opened her eyes and continued, "That's all I can see right now."

Sophia remembered that the last event on the itinerary was a pep rally at Treeville Middle School. She jumped up and walked fast to the desk in the room to see if the itinerary was still there.

She picked it up and said, "Tomorrow is the pep rally at Treeville. All the winners of the Disney competition will be led onto the field and given a salute before the game starts."

Sophia sat down at the desk and looked down at the itinerary for a few seconds. Then, she jumped up suddenly.

"We can do it tomorrow," Sophia said, with a clever smile. "After the pep rally, everyone will be watching the game, and no one will notice we're not there. It will be the perfect time to sneak back into the school."

Everyone's eyes widened with excitement. This would be their chance to destroy the alien and save the students at Treeville Middle School.

You could tell that Tycho was really thinking. Whenever he was deep in thought, he'd scratch his head. His thoughts turned toward Mr. Chuck's lab—a place that had every chemical imaginable on the shelves. Tycho thought if he could get back into Mr. Chuck's broom closet, next to the lab, he would have a place to create a piranha solution to bring Mr. Chuck down.

"That's it, I need to make a piranha solution," said Tycho.

Sophia asked, "What's a piranha solution? I hope it's not that stuff you made for the science fair with soap and dye."

Tycho cleared his throat before replying. "Piranha solution is a three to one mixture of concentrated sulfuric acid and 30% hydrogen peroxide. But if I add something like baking soda, acetone, or alcohol to the solution, it will be deadly."

Mya, Sophia, and Kyonn all looked at Tycho like he was speaking another language. Kyonn asked, "How deadly?"

"Combining all those chemicals will create skin burns," Tycho replied. "The solution can affect someone's breathing and eyesight, too. If we can put a lot of this stuff on Mr. Chuck, it will destroy him."

They knew if Mr. Chuck wasn't stopped, he would try to control the minds of all the kids at Treeville Middle School, just like he attempted to do with Sophia.

Kyonn was sitting on Mya's bed with his eyes closed. He was very still, which was unusual for him since he was always talking and moving, so Sophia got up from the sofa and walked over to Mya's bed.

"I can't believe you're sleeping right now!" Sophia yelled as she pushed Kyonn off the bed. He fell to the floor and sat up.

"Man, why you do that?" Kyonn said. "I wasn't asleep, I was just resting my eyes."

"Yeah, right," Sophia replied as she walked over to the sofa to sit next to Mya. "I think I heard you snoring."

"C'mon guys, I know it's late, but we need to have a plan for tomorrow," Mya said.

"Ok, let's go over this again, and I'm going to write it down this time," Sophia replied.

Tycho stood up. "I remember everything we just talked about, but I think we will need someone to cover for us when we leave the pep rally," he said. "What about Liv? She helped us before."

"I trust Liv," said Mya. "I can ask her to help when we get on the bus to go to the school."

They all agreed it would be a good idea to have a lookout, but they had to figure out how to get back into the school. Surely all the school's doors would be locked.

"Mya, who was the girl you met at the dance that goes to Treeville?" Kyonn asked. "Maybe she can tell us how to get back into the school and down to the basement?"

"Her name is Sarah," Mya replied. "We didn't exchange phone numbers so I will have to find her once we get to the pep rally."

Sophia walked around the room with a note pad and pen that she got off the nightstand in the bedroom.

"Ok, so here is the plan so far," she said. "We will meet everyone in the lobby. When we get on the bus, Mya will ask Liv to be our lookout. When we get to the school, Mya will ask Sarah to show us how to get back into the school." Sophia turned toward Mya. "Mya, once we are in the school, we will need you to see if Mr. Chuck is around so he doesn't catch us in his lab. If we are in the clear, we will go to the lab so Tycho can make the piranha."

"It is called piranha solution," Tycho replied.

Sophia gave Tycho a side-eye and continued, "Like I was saying, Tycho can make his potion and while he is doing that, we can look for other weapons in the lab that we can use to help stop Mr. Chuck. Mya, we will need you to tell us where to find Mr. Chuck. Once we see him, Tycho, you will have to strike him with your electricity to keep him still while Kyonn jumps from the building, leaps on his head, and injects the solution. Then, I will try and talk with him to see if we can get any information about their plan and why they are here."

"Well, it's getting late, and I'm not that confident about this plan," Tycho said. "Some of this we'll have to figure out as it is happening."

"I guess so," Mya said.

"We sure have a lot to do tomorrow, including destroying Mr. Chuck," said Sophia.

"We're going to need to get some sleep," said Kyonn. "See you guys at breakfast."

Tycho and Kyonn returned to their room for a good night's sleep.

Chapter 9

THE TAKEDOWN

Benjamin Lopez, Ann Taylor,
Dylan Turner, Kaylani Turner

"Today is the day," said Tycho.

While everyone was getting on the bus, Sophia put the paper from the notepad in her pocket. Tycho, Sophia, Kyonn, Liv, and Mya sat with each other on the bus. Kyonn started talking about the plan. Sophia told Kyonn to stop talking because she did not want anyone to hear.

As the bus pulled up to Treeville Middle School, some of the students were standing outside.

Mya, said, "Look, it's Sarah," and waved at her from the bus.

All the students ran off the bus. Mya, Tycho, Kyonn, Sophia, and Liv walked over to Sarah. Mya pulled her to the side and asked if she could show them a way into the school. Sarah said yes and told them to follow her. Sarah took them to the side door right next to the science lab. Mya said, "We've got it from here; we will see you at the pep rally."

The crew headed back to the football field to join the other students from Antluz Middle School for the Disney congratulatory walk around the field with the Disney characters. They were instructed to return to the bleachers once they left the field.

Mya turned to her friends and said, "Everyone looks very distracted. It's a perfect time for us to go."

As they walked toward the school, Tycho said, "It's time for us to stop this."

Mya, Liv, and Sarah were standing by the side door.

"I'm glad you were able to get us into the school," Mya said to Sarah. Then she turned to Liv and instructed her, "You stay here and make sure no one comes in. If you see a teacher or another student, make sure you slam the door or give a signal that someone is coming."

Mya and Liv shook hands, then Mya ran down the stairs in a hurry. As she walked into Mr. Chuck's closet, Sophia was standing by Tycho.

"Are you guys ready?" Mya asked. "We don't have much time."

Sophia and Mya were standing next to Tycho while he made his potion. Sophia said, "I can hear Mr. Chuck talking, like to an audience saying, 'This is the day we will rule the world.'" She could also hear little voices cheering.

Mya said, "I can see spots glowing. I can also see someone with one eye and a lot of arms."

Tycho asked Sophia if she could hear if there was more than one alien. Sophia said she could only hear noises. Tycho asked if Mya could see more than one alien and how tall they were. Mya said about six feet tall.

Tycho asked them to help him get all the items he needed for his potion. He rambled off the ingredients, barely taking a breath: "Mya and Sophia, go grab me those beakers, the big ones over there. Kyonn, grab me a lab coat. Sophia, can I have those safety goggles that are next to you and that yellow jar of acid? But don't shake it. Mya, grab that baking soda in the white jar and the hydrogen peroxide, sulfuric acid, and water. Kyonn, pass me those yellow gloves. Ok, thanks guys, this is everything I need. I need to focus so I can make this potion right the first time. Mya, I need a time check and update on where Mr. Chuck is."

"You got it, "Mya said.

While Tycho was making the potion, he instructed Kyonn to assemble the syringes and any weapons he could find.

Mya, "How much time do I have left? Where is Mr. Chuck?"

Mya closed her eyes and said, "I see him driving near all the stores we passed before the hotel. I see him stopping at a store to pick up some things but it's not clear what he is getting. My vision is blurry. Mr. Chuck is about twenty minutes away. He's in the car with four other people."

Mya asked Sophia if she could hear anything. Sophia could hear them saying they needed to get back to the school and prepare. Mya turned around and saw the computer with pictures of students including the crew. The photos were labeled Protocol 8772. Sophia could hear Mr. Chuck saying he was coming to activate Protocol 8772 and needed to return to the lab.

Kyonn said with urgency, "Hurry up, Tycho, Mya said we don't have much time. We have twenty minutes to get everything together and get into position."

Rather gloomily, Sophia said, "The noises are getting louder which means they are getting closer."

"Alright, I'm done," Tycho said. "Kyonn, you have five minutes to put the potion into the syringes."

Kyonn grabbed a pair of gloves for protection and began to fill all the syringes with the piranha solution.

"Let's go," said Tycho.

"We will cut him off in the back of the school. We can't let him get to the lab," said Mya.

As they all turned around to leave, a loud noise came from upstairs.

"That must be Liv. Someone is coming," said Mya.

"Okay, it's time to stop Protocol 8772," said Kyonn.

With wide eyes and hearts pounding, the crew approached the back door. As they opened it, Mr. Chuck was getting out of his car. He looked human, but he was mumbling something that didn't sound like any language they had heard before.

They ambushed him as Sophia shouted, "We will destroy you and Protocol 8772."

The four friends surrounded Mr. Chuck as he looked at them with admiration and pity. "You fools!" he said. "You can't destroy me. If I were you, I'd leave right now before it's too late."

Mya said, "Everyone, stay in your position and be ready to attack!"

It was then, right before their eyes, that Mr. Chuck transformed into an alien. He had shimmering green scales, large yellow eyes with a streak of neon blue, long arms, and two webbed feet. The crew moved back three feet and looked at each other.

Mya screamed, "NOW!!!"

Tycho hit the smaller aliens with electricity and Mya sprayed the potion on them. They fell and started shaking.

Mya yelled, "Watch out, he is coming from the left."

Tycho turned around and put his hands out. He hit Mr. Chuck with his electricity and yelled, "You're going down, Mr. Chuck!"

"Hold him still with your electricity," Kyonn said as he jumped on the side of the building, then on top of the building, then crashed down on Mr. Chuck's head with several syringes in hand.

Kyonn injected Mr. Chuck with the potion three times then jumped down to the ground.

They watched Mr. Chuck fall to his knees with his eyes bulging and his skin pulsating. He seemed dazed and confused. He shook his ugly head back and forth as if trying to shake it off. But then it was like he got a burst of energy. The potion was not as effective as they had hoped, and Mr. Chuck stood back up a little unsteadily.

Mya screamed, "Oh no, it's not working! We should probably get out of…"

But before she could finish her sentence, with the speed of a gazelle, one of Mr. Chuck's arms grabbed her, squeezed her, and held her in the air like she was a hot air balloon.

The kids were stunned but couldn't give up now.

Sophia screamed at the alien, "Put her down right now you evil being!"

He laughed a hideous laugh and said, "What was that injection? Some science fair project gone wrong? I told you to leave me alone, but you and your meddling friends are now going to pay the price."

Tycho was insulted that Mr. Chuck basically called his potion trash. He was determined to show him it wasn't!

"Everyone, grab a syringe. We are going to inject him at the same time," Tycho said.

"Now!" screamed Sophia.

They all charged at Mr. Chuck, poking him with the needles repeatedly.

Mr. Chuck's body started shaking and foam was coming from his mouth. His arms swung around like spaghetti, and his eyes were wide while his body started melting. As his arms shrunk, Mya came closer to the ground until she was released and dropped with a thud, scraping her hands and knees.

The crew stood there staring at what was now a blob of green-looking snot.

At first, they were silent. No one would ever believe they conquered an alien. None of them had used a phone to take a picture or anything to prove it existed, but that didn't matter. They knew what they had done, and they were proud.

"We did it!" screamed Sophia.

They all jumped up and down, yelling, screaming, and giving each other high fives. Soon the blob was just a puddle.

While they were celebrating, a loud voice said, "That was so cool!"

When they turned around, Liv and Sarah were standing there cheering them on. The crew knew it wasn't good that Liv and Sarah saw everything, so Mya walked up to them.

"Look into my eyes," she told them.

When they did, there was a spark of light.

Then Mya asked them, "What did you just see?"

Liv answered, seeming confused, "Nothing. I mean, I can't remember."

Mya was satisfied that her two friends no longer remembered seeing them destroy Mr. Chuck. Then Mr. Mohammed came in from the bleachers.

He ran up to the crew and asked, "Are you guys ok? What just happened here?"

With hesitation, Sophia explained, "Well, while walking to the restroom, I saw lights coming from the janitor's room closet that looked similar to the stuff in the jar on the top shelf of your lab. I was curious. When I entered the janitor's closet, I saw him turn into an alien"

Tycho jumped in proudly saying, "And I made the piranha solution that killed him."

Mr. Mohammed stood there with his hands on his hips looking at them back and forth as if watching a tennis match. Before they could continue, he abruptly stopped them from explaining and said, "Let's go back to the pep rally and we will talk further about what just happened when we are back at school."

Chapter 10

HOME SWEET HOME

Benjamin Lopez, Ann Taylor,
Dylan Turner, Kaylani Turner

The next morning, the crew woke up at 6:30 a.m. and went downstairs to get the continental breakfast.

When they sat down at the table, Tycho said, "Can you believe we destroyed Mr. Chuck?"

"Yeah, I can," said Kyonn. "My hands still hurt from last night."

"My arms feel like spaghetti arms," said Tycho.

"My head hurts and I feel a slight pain on my right side," said Mya.

"My ears feel weird. It's like a constant ringing," said Sophia.

For the rest of the trip, the kids were inseparable. Only when they were together in private did they talk about the alien and how they probably saved the world. On the bus ride back, it was hard not to discuss it, so they busied themselves with games, their phones, reading, and other activities.

When they got back to the school parking lot, Mr. Greg was standing with a sign that read "Welcome Back Antluz Middle School." The other students exited the bus, but Mya, Tycho, Sophia, and Kyonn were the last to leave.

Mya was smiling and moving around as if listening to music only she could hear.

"Well, that was one amazing adventure. I hope we don't have to do anything like that again," she said.

"You can say that again," Tycho said in agreement. "And Sophia next time don't wander off by yourself, okay?"

Sophia smiled. "I know right. But you guys saved me. I'm so grateful for all of you."

They gave each other a group hug.

"Hey, I checked earlier and my superpowers are gone. What about the rest of you?" Kyonn questioned.

"When that alien died, did our powers die too?" asked Tycho.

Mya responded, "I believe we still have them, but we can only use them if danger is present. And don't ask me how I know that. I just do!"

They agreed that was for the best, then the bus driver was suddenly among them.

"Okay, kids, let's go. Time to get off the bus. How was your trip?"

They all spoke at once about the good time they had, never mentioning the alien.

Mr. Bushmen said, "Glad to hear it. You know, if you follow all the protocols, things usually go as planned."

At the word "protocol," the kids stopped in their tracks staring at Mr. Bushmen.

Tycho blinked, leaned in, and asked, "What did you say?"

Mr. Bushmen smiled at them. "Oh, nothing. Y'all come on off of here. I have other things I need to do."

The crew hurried off the bus quietly, lost in the moment, each thinking the same thing but not wanting to revisit it ever again.

Mr. Mohammed stayed behind and seemed to have words with the bus driver. Had the kids looked back, they would have seen both of their eyes glowing yellow with neon blue streaks.

ABOUT THE AUTHORS

Benjamin Lopez

 Ten-year-old Benjamin Lopez was born in Maryland and later moved to York County, Pennsylvania. At an early age, Benjamin showed an interest in mathematics. He excelled in math and was therefore inducted into the gifted and talented program of the Baltimore County Public School system. Later, he achieved the same distinction in the Southern York County School District in Pennsylvania.

Benjamin loves playing goalie in his soccer league. He enjoys writing stories and even created a YouTube channel with his sister Audrey called The New Style Kids where they create short-form content like short films and instructional videos. Benjamin also enjoys building things and playing with Legos. He wants to become a scientist when he grows up.

Ann Taylor

Ann Elizabeth Taylor is an eleven-year-old, sixth-grade honor roll student at a Baltimore County middle school. She is a kind-hearted, fun-loving young lady. Ann has a passion for drawing and painting, which she intends to pursue further throughout her educational journey.

Dylan Turner

Dylan Turner is an eleven-year-old fifth-grader. He likes to play video games, basketball, and football. He also loves to swim. Dylan plays drums and is in the band at his school. He is an assistant drummer at his church and is on the junior usher board. Dylan uses his library card to borrow anime books, like the My Hero Academia manga series, and he also enjoys drawing.

Kaylani Turner

Kaylani Turner is a curious and energetic fifth-grade elementary school student who has a love for learning and exploring. Kaylani brightens up every classroom with enthusiasm and kindness.

She is always eager to dive into new adventures, whether it's through reading books or playing sports with friends on the playground. When Kaylani is not busy with school, you can find her drawing, riding her bike, or spending time with her family and pet dog. Kaylani continues to grow, learn, and spread joy to everyone around her.

publish your gift

CREATING DISTINCTIVE BOOKS
FOR LEADERS AT THE TOP OF THEIR FIELD

We're a collaborative group of creative masterminds
with a mission to empower leaders to share their unique
knowledge, insights, and experiences with the world.

Our expertise bridges the gap between
their wisdom and ideal readers—delivering impactful
self-help books that inspire lasting growth and change.

Want to know more?
Write to us at info@publishyourgift.com
or call (888) 949-6228

Discover great books, authors, and more at
www.PublishYourGift.com

Connect with us on social media

@publishyourgift